THE COWBOY'S CHRISTMAS STAR

THE CHRISTMAS STAR COLLECTION BOOK ONE

EDITH MACKENZIE

May all your Christmases be special

THREE MONTHS TILL CHRISTMAS

Good Lord, she was tired. Veronica couldn't remember the last time she'd had more than a day off, let alone a single day off. She tried not to complain. She was living every actress who came to Tinseltown's dream. But after coming off eight back-to-back movies, the last one about sex trafficking had sapped the last of her creative energies.

"I have a message from Anton," her agent's assistant said as Veronica sunk exhaustedly into the chair. "He asked me to give it to you when you came in to see Herb."

Herb waved for his assistant to continue. Clearing her throat, she glanced nervously around before reading from the note. "My dearest Veronica." Again, the assistant looked down at her boss. "Maybe I could just give it to Veronica, and she can read it herself in private."

"I'm her agent. She doesn't have anything private from me," Herb barked. "Now, get on with it."

Again, she cleared her throat. "What we have is special." Veronica smiled. Anton was a sweetheart and the perfect fiancé. Since they'd become a couple a year ago, they'd been quite the celebrity pairing. That is, when they were in the same country. When had they last been in the same country? She couldn't remember.

"Um, I adore you, but it isn't working out for me. I hope we can continue to love and have the upmost respect for each other."

Veronica's stomach churned. "I don't understand."

"He's broken up with you, Veronica. Deal with it. We have movies to make." Herb rifled through the scripts on his desk. "Did you read the romcom I sent you?"

Veronica stared, uncomprehending. "Anton broke up with me? He promised to spend Christmas with me this year."

Herb gave her a cynical look. "Who cares about Christmas anyway?"

"I do!" Veronica jumped to her feet. "I do. And you and Anton and everyone else can go take a giant leap!"

THE SMOG LOOKED as though it was smothering LA. It seemed fitting, like it was trying to extinguish all the hopes and dreams that Tinseltown fed on. Veronica rubbed delicately at her eyes, careful not to damage the skin. One could never be too careful, especially when her face was what had made her fortune—that and her body. At least, that's what she'd been told since she was sixteen years old and appeared in her first feature film. She shuddered thinking about the handsy director whispering in her ear about everything she could have if only she did him this one favor.

Veronica pulled herself away from the edge of darkness, inhaling a shaky breath. Desperately, she cast her gaze around the living room, Anton's belongings mingling with hers. The paparazzi were already gathered outside like vultures attracted to the smell of fresh blood. She wanted to throw things and scream, but that wasn't the sort of person she was. Instead, she pushed it down, drawing it deep inside of her. He was a coward, breaking the news while he was away, leaving her to deal with the fallout. But then, he'd left her to deal with everything that wasn't perfect their entire relationship. Maybe if she'd ever experienced a normal relationship in her life, she'd have known this wasn't love. This feeling thrashing around inside of her, maybe it wasn't heartbreak. Perhaps it was just the loss of a fantasy she'd built up in her head and the blow to her ego. Blowing her nose, she sat down on the heinously expensive sofa, the one Anton had insisted on. Not terribly comfortable, but had the right price tag and name attached to it.

Breathe, Veronica, this is nothing but a moment in time. Giving up on the sofa providing any solace, she abandoned it. She had scripts to read. That was one thing Anton couldn't take from her. Veronica Hughes was a movie star, with or without him.

Suzie quickly pushed through the door, Veronica slamming it shut before the media could get a glimpse of her. Even with living in the gated community with the high fence around her property, pictures were still finding their way into magazines. She still wasn't sure how the ones from when the removalist had come to take Anton's things away had managed to show the inside of her house. The day she'd found them, she'd felt violated. Frankly, the sooner the next scandal of the month happened to someone else the better.

"You know, I've always had a thing for minimalist styling." Suzie pushed back her neon green hair as she looked around. "Is it wrong that this place seems nicer since Anton left?"

Veronica perched herself on a bar stool at her kitchen bench, pouring them both a generous glass of wine. "I should arrange for an interior designer to come over and redo it all, but I just can't be bothered." She passed Suzie a glass before taking a sip of her own. "And wouldn't the press have a field day with that. Lonely Veronica seeks comfort in redecorating her empty house." Self-pity soured the wine in her mouth.

"Or Veronica Hughes is removing that man right out of her life and with style." Suzie laughed before gazing at her friend earnestly. "You guys never really spent longer than two weeks together."

"We had busy careers." Veronica hunched defensively over the marble counter, cradling her drink. "It's hard to be in the same country at times, let alone the same house."

Suzie smiled sympathetically at her, her red false eyelashes brushing her rounded cheeks. "All I'm saying is that if you'd lived together like a proper couple for a chunk of time, would you have lasted as long as you did? I mean, I hate to say it, but the man is vain and narcissistic. He was punching way above his weight both in terms of the amazing human being you are and as far as the star power you have compared to him. You were and still are way out of his league." Seeing she had Veronica's attention, she paused, raising a considering brow at her. "Maybe, in the long term, him calling off the engagement isn't such a bad thing."

Veronica sucked in a breath, drawing herself up to her full seated height, prepared to protest Suzie's words, to rant how wrong she was, and then it struck her. The idea that had been whispering at her the whole time crystalized. Her friend had verbalized exactly what she'd been feeling but had been too caught up in self-pity, embarrassment and hurt pride to acknowledge it.

"You might"—she held up a finger to stop her friend's satisfied smirk—"and I'm only admitting to might, have a point." A helicopter buzzing around the house drew both of their attention to the large glass picture window. "But he's still a jerk for leaving me here with no warning to deal with it."

"You're not going to get any argument from me on that point. I thought he was a jerk long before this."

Veronica laughed at her friend's vicious smile. "Thanks

for saying something earlier."

"You didn't want to hear it, and I wouldn't ruin our friendship by saying it to you." The palms outside thrashed around in the wind whipped up by the helicopter. "It's ridiculous that they're still trying to get pictures of you." A devilish gleam came over her pixie features. "But if it's pictures they want…" Setting her glass down, she strode over to the window. Veronica could only watch mystified. *What on earth is she doing?* With a deft wiggle, Suzie dropped her pants and pressed her backside against the glass. "Let them take a picture of that!"

Veronica erupted in horrified laughter at her friend's daring. "They might think it's me!"

Looking smugly pleased with herself, Suzie pulled her pants back up. "You wish your backside looked as good as this."

Great peals of laughter erupted from her, convulsing her body at Suzie's sass. "A girl can dream." *Gosh, it felt good to let go of all the tension and misery she'd wrapped herself up in.* Coming to a sudden decision, Veronica banged her fist on the table, wincing in regret when she did it with more vigor than she'd planned. "That's it. I'm not spending a minute longer here than I already have. And definitely not Christmas. You coming?"

Suzie settled back beside her at the bench, a bemused expression on her face. "You haven't even told me where we're going."

"I haven't decided yet. Are you coming or not?" A spark set a fire in her belly.

Suzie raised her glass. "Of course I'm coming. If only to give the paps something to snap."

Veronica clinked her glass against her friend's. "Then it's settled. Girls Christmas, here we come." *At least once I figure out where.*

"Ma'am, are you sure a ranch in Wyoming is the thing for you?" The elderly gentleman looked like he was about to have a stroke. Veronica tried not to smile too obviously. There was a respectful concern to him that didn't get her hackles up the way her agent's sneering condescension had when she'd informed him of her plans.

"I'm sure it can't be that hard, and what I don't know, I'm sure we'll"—she gestured between her and Suzie, resplendent in a black tutu and leggings—"figure it out."

"Speak for yourself," Suzie murmured. "I plan on sitting near that open fire you showed me in the pictures, roasting chestnuts and sipping mulled wine. Frankly, I don't anticipate leaving that position until New Year's."

"But there's stock," protested the real estate broker, Marvin. "Ma'am, I don't feel comfortable selling this property to you without someone knowing what's what. It just ain't right. I wouldn't be able to sleep with myself at night." He stopped short, looking at the two mulish expressions across the table from him, his words like a red rag to a bull. "Um. But I might know a fella willing to come out and help run it for you. He's been helping me with some odd jobs about town. He's reliable and knows what he's doing, and I bet he'd be willing to stay in the staff quarters you have on the property as part payment."

Veronica pressed her lips together. Marvin did have a point. It might seem like the best Christmas idea ever to buy a ranch and have a white Christmas, but maybe it wasn't terribly practical. After all, what did they actually know about ranching? Suzie could put makeup on all the cows, and she could give them acting lessons, she supposed. She held out her hand. "Deal. Make him a fair offer for his time and include the accommodation."

Relief washed over Marvin's features as he accepted her hand. "I'm glad we could come to an agreement. I'll send him over once you gals are settled."

Satisfied, she looked down at their joined hands, the signed sales contract on the desk beneath them. *Veronica Hughes, the movie star, could now add ranch owner to her resume.* Excited, she grinned at Suzie. "Ready to go see our ranch?"

Suzie leapt to her feet. "I thought you'd never ask. And now it comes with its very own cowboy! I think I'm about to pop."

Veronica didn't care that much about the man coming to help—as long as he did his job. All she wanted was a nice Christmas, and that's what she planned on getting.

Snow dusted everything. The rolling hills and meadows that Veronica imagined were covered in grass in summer were now pristine in their winter adornment. Deep tree-covered canyons cut through the landscape as they drove toward the main lodge on the ranch.

Suzie was thumbing through the sales advert. "It says here that it has two heated helicopter pads. I guess that will make it convenient to fly back to LA if the notion strikes you."

"Or easier for Santa's reindeer to land." Veronica was starting to get excited. Buying this ranch, being here, it was just what she needed.

"I hadn't thought of the poor reindeer. At least they can warm up while Santa makes his delivery."

Veronica gripped the steering wheel as they got closer to the log cabin rising majestically above them overlooking a pond and then out over the expanse of land before it. Everything about it screamed home to her. "We're here."

"I'm feeling this," Suzie said, gazing through the windscreen with her. "I didn't want to say anything, but reading that this place has over six thousand acres and all the stuff on it, I'm glad old Marvin insisted that we get someone who knows what they're doing to help. I'm not sure we could do it on our own."

Veronica clicked the buzzer and the garage door opened. Slowly, she pulled the car in. "I think it was the right decision too. And the best bit is, it leaves us to enjoy our holiday."

"Quick question." Suzie waved a finger about in the air. "Do the holidays officially start now?"

"As soon as we get our bags to our rooms."

"And then what?"

"I have a plan."

Suzie grinned at her. "I think it's the same one I have. Ready?"

Veronica rested her hand on the door handle, ready to open it. "And three, two, one. Go!"

In a surprisingly short amount of time, both girls were back downstairs. "What now?" Suzie asked, pushing back her neon locks.

Veronica grinned and threw an apron at her. "We bake."

Suzie grinned back at her as she caught it. "And what are we baking?"

"Sugar cookies."

"Any theme?"

"Winter wonderland." Veronica began to open cupboards, looking for baking equipment. "But first we need to get the lay of the land." A buzz on her phone alerted her to another message from Herb no doubt asking when she'd be back.

Suzie firmly reached out and took it from her hand. "Herb and anyone else for that matter can wait."

Knowing that she was right, Veronica found some music to play. As an upbeat melody sounded, they got to work, laughing and dancing as they baked up a storm in the kitchen. LA felt a lifetime ago. "Don't tell Herb about all the calories."

"I don't intend on telling Herb anything, odious little man that he is." Suzie placed her decorated cookie down on the plate. Veronica wasn't really sure that purple and green candy canes fit the theme of winter wonderland, but each to their own. She'd decided to go with baby blue and white snowflakes. A sharp knock on the door interrupted their domestic bliss. "Are you expecting anyone?"

Veronica shook her head. "The whole point of being out here is to not be expecting anyone."

"I'll go see who it is, just in case the media have found out that you're here." Suzie pulled a wicked face. "And then I'll send them on their way."

Veronica couldn't help laughing as her friend scuttled away, doing her best wicked stepmother impersonation. Trying to keep out of sight, she could hear a man's low rumbling baritone. "Veronica, it's all clear. You can come out," Suzie called.

Curious, she complied, setting her last cookie down on the plate before wiping her hands on the front of her apron. Stepping out from the kitchen into the living room, she stopped dead in her tracks. Just inside the front door was the most gorgeous cowboy she'd ever seen and a cute little girl. Everything about him screamed rugged manliness. The way he stood with his feet braced, pulling the denim on his thighs snug. His broad shoulders filling his jacket. The way he twisted the brim of his hat in his hands. And then he looked up at her with chocolate brown eyes set into a tanned, strong face. Veronica swallowed. *Is it getting hot in here?*

IT WAS clear from what the girls were wearing that they were exactly what Marvin had said on the phone—city girls with more money than sense. Although Marvin had said that they were a class act, especially the one who had purchased the ranch, Veronica, the movie star. Personally, Hank thought maybe old Marvin had been a little starstruck. An actress had no business buying a ranch in Wyoming, especially not in winter. *Do they even know one end of a steer from another, let alone the difference between cattle and bison? And this time of year? The weather can be harsh. I reckon they think they're in some sort of mushy Christmas movie. But the blonde sure is a looker.*

"This gentleman was just telling me that Marvin sent him over—the ranch hand he told us about." The girl who had answered the door, her hair a bright neon green, smiled at him. She looked like some sort of manic pixie, but seemed nice enough. "But no one told us about this cute extra hand." She winked down at Lulu.

Hank rested his hand reassuringly on his daughter's shoulder. At just turned three, she could still be timid around strangers. "I'm Hank, and this is Lulu. Marvin mentioned that accommodation was included in the job. I hope having my daughter stay with me won't be a problem." He didn't mean to sound so defensive, but he needed this job—for the both of them.

The blonde stepped closer, smiling warmly, her hand extended. "I'm Veronica, and yes, it is." Her eyes were friendly as she looked down at Lulu. "And of course your daughter is welcome."

Hank was surprised at the businesslike grip of her handshake. He'd been expecting something hesitant. "When do you want me to start?"

"You can start as soon as you want. Do you need some time to get your things settled into the ranch quarters?" Veronica asked.

"Lulu and I travel light. If it's all right with you, I reckon we can get settled tonight and be ready to start tomorrow."

Suzie knelt down in front of Lulu. "Would you like some

cookies? They're fresh from the oven and the icing might have even set a little by now."

His daughter's face lit up at the mention of treats and she looked hesitantly up at him, unsure yet if it would be okay. He gave her shoulder another gentle squeeze. "If it isn't an inconvenience," he said.

"How could this little cutie be an inconvenience?" Suzie ushered his daughter into the kitchen.

Lulu quickly scoffed down the plate of cookies that were set in front of her, washing it down with a glass of milk all while chattering away to her new friend. Guilt twisted inside of him. How long had it been since he'd last offered her something to eat? They'd had a hearty breakfast and then some sandwiches at lunch, but clearly the kid was hungry. *I really need to make sure I pack snacks.* Lulu seemed at ease with the two women. Maybe she was missing having female company. If you didn't count Didi at the diner, she hadn't had much since her mom had up and decided she wasn't cut out to be a parent anymore.

"Did Marvin go over what the job entailed?" Veronica topped up his coffee.

"He said that you were first-time ranchers and that, given the stock this place has on it, you needed some help."

"Poor Marvin looked like he was having a stroke when I told him I wanted to buy this place." She took a nibble from a cookie, crumbs sticking to her bottom lip before her tongue darted out and captured them. For a moment, Hank forgot what they were talking about.

"Marvin's a bit of an old busybody. But his heart is in the right place and he sure has helped me out."

"I assume he talked wages with you?"

There was something warm and direct about her that he hadn't been expecting. Hank got the sense that she didn't beat around the bush. He actually quite liked her. Still didn't mean that it was the smartest idea for her to be out here buying a ranch. "He did, but I thought you might want to go over it again."

She waved his suggestion away as she reached for another cookie. "I'm sure Marvin offered you a fair deal." She quirked a brow at him. "Unless you don't think he did?"

"No, ma'am. Marvin is fair."

Veronica smiled, dimples dancing to life in her cheeks. "Excellent. Then it sounds like we have a deal. Welcome to working for me."

Hank pushed himself away from the table and took his plate to the sink. "Lulu, it's time we go get ourselves settled." He tried not to see his daughter's bottom lip drop.

Veronica smiled brightly at the little girl. "Lulu, since you're going to be just over the way now, you can come visit anytime you want."

"So can the father," murmured Suzie.

Amused, Hank watched a slightly flustered Veronica give her friend a warning glare to behave herself—one that was clearly ignored. Gathering his daughter, he began to wonder if this might be an interesting Christmas after all.

Hank had to admit there was something appealingly cute about watching Veronica climb back into his truck in her padded overalls, jacket, and thick boots. So far, she hadn't complained once about getting out at each and every gate they stopped at. *Maybe I should start taking the more direct route and save her the effort ... nah.*

"So, this paddock is the one that has the bison in it?" she asked as she settled herself back into her seat.

"Yes, ma'am. Your ranch mostly runs cattle, but the last owner put a thousand acres to bison. The wooded areas are stocked with elk as well." He liked that she asked questions, storing the information away. She might be a delicate blonde city girl, but she was smart and not afraid to get her hands dirty. A dangerously appealing combination as far as he was concerned.

"I feel silly that there's so much I didn't know when I bought the ranch. I guess I knew there was stock—the ad said so, and Marvin made a big song and dance about it—but now that I'm actually responsible for the lives of these creatures ... well." Veronica turned the full force of her cornflower blue eyes onto him. "I'm grateful that he insisted we have you here and that you accepted."

Hank plumb forgot how to breathe under the power of her admiring gaze. It sure had been a while since he'd felt like anything but a failure. He cleared his throat. "I appreciate you having us here and Suzie watching Lulu for me while I work. It sure does make the day a little easier with not having to keep an eye on her."

"I'm not sure who enjoys it more, Suzie or Lulu." An easy smile played at the corners of her generous mouth. "I do worry about how much trouble the pair of them could get into left unattended."

"You don't have to come with me every day, or at all if you prefer." Each morning she'd met him in the barn, ready to spend the day with him. If the thought of her not being there tomorrow left him feeling lonesome, well, that was just because he'd gotten used to her being around. "I can manage."

"I want to learn. Seriously, how do you know all of this stuff—and especially about my ranch?"

"It helps that I grew up in the area. In fact, you see over there?" An iced-over creek barely peeped from beneath a cover of snow.

She peered through the windscreen, following his gaze. "I think so."

"That creek there has some of the best trout fishing in the county. Brown and rainbow. In summer there's no better way to spend a lazy afternoon but fly fishing with a little music and a picnic blanket spread out." In fact, he'd had his first kiss on the banks of that creek. Hank didn't think he needed to tell Veronica that little piece of information. It didn't help that his head filled with visions of kissing one Veronica Hughes on a spread-out blanket beneath a wide-open blue sky

"That sounds amazing." Hank's blood beat faster in his ears. Thank God she didn't know what he was thinking about. "Lulu would love that."

Her words were like a bucket of cold water bringing him back to reality. "I reckon she would."

"I'll be gone by then, but I was thinking I'd like for you to stay on year-round to manage it if that's acceptable. I know you'll look after it like your own."

Hank was hit by more emotions than he had a right to be feeling. At the forefront was gratitude and relief. Lulu would have somewhere to call home, and he'd be able to provide for her. Underneath that layer was something he didn't want to probe too much, a hollowness at how casually she tossed out that she would be leaving. Of course she would leave. She was a movie star. Why would she stay in this little hick town? Why did he even have an opinion on it anyway? He'd only just met the woman. And a glow that she wanted him to look after it for her. "I'd like that, ma'am."

Veronica turned those blue eyes back to him with full force. "And that's another thing. Call me Veronica or Ronny, but please stop calling me ma'am. It just seems a little impersonal if you're going to be looking after my ranch for me. That, or I should have gray hair and wrinkles."

"I think I can do that ... Veronica." Darn if her name didn't feel good on his tongue. He made a show of looking at her closely. "Don't reckon there's a gray hair or wrinkle in sight." She laughed, low and throaty. It was sexy as all heck. Deciding he'd played with enough fire for the day, he turned the wheel. "There are some things I need to do back at the barn, and I know a shortcut back to the lodge." He gave her a wicked look. "You might want to hold on."

GLITTER, card, twine, and pinecones were strewn about the kitchen table, Christmas carols playing in the background. Veronica tried not to laugh at the earnest expression—each mirrored by the other—on Suzie and Lulu's faces as they worked. She'd shed her outer layer in the mudroom before entering the kitchen, pausing to enjoy the impossible cuteness in front of her. She smiled warmly up at the handsome cowboy beside her.

"I think they might be having fun," she whispered.

"I find with Lulu, the bigger the mess, the more she enjoyed it."

"You know we can hear you, right?" Suzie called without taking her eyes off her handiwork.

"We didn't want to disturb you," retorted Veronica, fully making her way into the room. She held the coffee pot out to Hank in question.

He gave her a nod before turning his attention to his daughter. "What ya making there, Lulu?"

"Corniments," the little girl replied seriously, holding out her handiwork.

"Corniments?" Hank gave Suzie a questioning look.

"Ornaments," she clarified. "Lulu and I thought we might start getting into the Christmas spirit."

"Oh, I see." Hank took the pinecone from his daughter. "Lulu, I don't reckon I've ever seen a more glittery pinecone in my life."

"She's got a lot of fabulousness," Suzie said proudly, touching the side of her neon green hair, today scraped up into a faux mohawk. It now sparkled under the lights, mute testament to having touched it with glitter encrusted hands at some point.

"That she does," agreed Hank as he accepted the steaming cup of coffee from Veronica. "I think I might have lost my little offsider."

"Veronica makes a good replacement," Suzie murmured, taking the coffee pot from Veronica, ready to pour her own cup. "And I'm sure she'd be keen to be hands-on."

Veronica gave her friend a warning glare, not that it ever did much good. "Will Lulu's mom be visiting for Christmas?"

Hank's expression turned frigid. "I doubt it. She isn't in the picture anymore and that's her decision." His tone shut down that line of questioning immediately. *That woman must have broken his heart.* Pity filled her. *Poor Hank.* "What about you? Are you expecting any special guests for Christmas?"

Veronica blinked, caught off-balance by him throwing a personal question back at her. Did he care if she did? "I've just come out of a relationship. It ended suddenly. So, no."

He sent her a piercing look as if trying to see if she'd had her heart broken like his. The strangest part of it all was, as they sat in the cozy kitchen sipping coffee, homemade crafts between them, Veronica wondered again if she'd ever cared enough about Anton for him to break her heart at all. Strange how, once she'd gotten away from LA, everything she'd thought was so real was beginning to feel like nothing more than cardboard cutouts and special effects.

FOUR WEEKS TILL CHRISTMAS

Two short weeks was all it had taken to fall into the natural rhythm of life on the ranch. Veronica knew Hank didn't need her help, but she liked to greet him in the morning with a hot cup of coffee when he dropped Lulu off and talk about his plans for the day. Sometimes he'd ask her to come along if he thought it was something she'd like to see or do. His consideration of her always set a warm glow flickering in her belly. There was never an over-the-top gesture or flowery language, just a steady regard.

Ready to begin setting the table for dinner, Veronica headed for the kitchen, pausing as she heard Suzie and Lulu having a whispered conversation. At least, Suzie whispered, and Lulu listened.

"Wouldn't it be a Christmas miracle if they fell in love?" Suzie said to her pint-sized companion. "She deserves to be happy."

"I'm happy as it is. I'm not sure I need to rush into falling in love," Veronica protested, enjoying the way Suzie jumped guiltily. "Even if I do think Hank is … nice."

"Nice? That's such a beige way to describe that hunk of a

cowboy. He's like this perfect gentleman with his manners and treating a lady all respectful, but you just know that, underneath those snug jeans, he's pure man." Suzie winked at her. "If you know what I mean."

"A simpleton knows what you mean. You're not exactly subtle."

"I know you've noticed, and I also know that you've noticed he has a bit of a crush on you and, as your friend, all I'm saying is that I think you don't mind at all."

"What doesn't she mind?" This time it was Veronica's turn to jump guiltily when Hank's voice rumbled behind her. Suzie grinned at her mischievously. *Some friend.*

"Would you like to tell Hank, or would you like me to?" her green-haired friend asked innocently.

Turning, Veronica decided to take matters into her own hands. There was no way she was trusting Suzie to not say something embarrassing. Her gaze drifted for a moment to those snug jeans before she jerked her mind back to safer territory. "We were just talking about how things have been going since we got here and that we like it. That we don't mind it at all." She tried to ignore the snort from behind her. Hank quirked a brow, looking over her shoulder, but clearly chose to ignore it otherwise. "Now, I was just about to set the table, if you'd like to wash up for dinner."

After a dinner of roast chicken and vegetables—*Hollywood diets could go take a leap*—Suzie shooed them out on the pretense of doing the dishes since Veronica cooked, and insisted that after a hard day working the ranch, she wouldn't allow Hank to help her.

"I guess we should do what she says," Hank said with a rueful roll of his broad shoulders.

"When she's in a mood like this, it's best to just stay out of her way," Veronica agreed, leading them into the living room where a fire flickered moodily, casting a warm glow over the room.

Veronica took a seat on the sofa. Surprised, she bit down on her lower lip when Hank took the spot beside her instead of on the opposite sofa. He wasn't exactly touching her, but she could feel the way his body filled up the space. Lulu stood in front of Veronica until she held her arms out for the child to climb onto her lap. Veronica didn't think her heart could take how full it felt in that moment.

"She really seems to have taken to you." Hank smiled down at his already drowsy daughter.

"I think Suzie is her favorite."

"The way you both have opened your home to her, I can't thank you enough. The last few months have been hard on her."

Veronica could feel Lulu's breathing slowing down as she slipped into sleep. Her chest squeezed in a painfully pleasant way. There was something about a child feeling safe enough to drift off that made a person feel special. She'd always wanted children, but there had never seemed to be the right time. Herb always had another movie lined up, and Anton wasn't keen on the disruption a child would have had on their globe-trotting lifestyle. She glanced toward Hank, touched by the moment.

∾

EYES SHINING, Veronica looked at him as if her soul was swimming in the depths of her gaze. "How could Lulu's mother not want to be a part of this?"

His stomach twisted, part guilt, part anger. "I used to be a rodeo rider and I lived that lifestyle to the hilt, something I'm not proud of now. Lulu wasn't planned. In fact, she was the result of a one-night stand. But I never denied she was my responsibility and I provided for her and her mother, which meant being on the circuit and not seeing her as much as I wanted. But every chance I got, I spent it with my baby girl. Molly didn't seem to care if I was there or not. She just wanted the money I could give her, and she certainly was happy with what I could earn from rodeos." There was a sourness in the pit of his stomach, a heaviness that nagged at him like an old wound. "I thought I was doing the right thing."

The gentle touch of her hand on his was nearly his undoing. "I'm sure you were doing everything you could."

"A few months ago, Molly knocked on my motel door out of the blue and handed Lulu over with a tiny suitcase of her belongings. Said she didn't want to be a mother anymore." His bitterness threatened to choke him. "That it wasn't the life she wanted for herself." He breathed down the rage roaring to life inside of him. "The next day, I quit the circuit —that's no life for a little girl—and I came home. I was doing odd jobs around town for Marvin when he called me to help here and the rest"—he gave her a little smile—"as they say, is history."

Veronica still hadn't taken her hand away from his, the warmth of it anchoring him to the moment. "I can't imagine this ranch without you or Lulu here. And I know that sounds like I'm flaky with only knowing you both for such a short time, but it's true."

Staring into her glorious eyes, how could Hank tell her that being at this ranch with her had filled a hole he didn't know needed filling? She would think he was one heck of an operator if he came out with that line. After only two weeks, no less! Lulu shifted on Veronica's lap, giving a little murmuring sigh, breaking the moment.

"I should probably get Lulu to bed."

"She's all tuckered out from trying to keep up with Suzie.

Trust me, Suzie is a hard act to follow." Veronica gently tucked a stray hair behind the girl's ear.

Hank gathered his slumbering daughter into his arms, still as light as a feather. He wondered when she would seem heavy or if she would always be his little girl, no matter how old she got. "Thank you for dinner tonight—and every night."

The even whiteness of her smile was dazzling. "We love having you eat dinner with us, and it doesn't seem right for you to have to go back to your quarters and make something for you and Lulu after working all day." Her expression softened as she gazed down at Lulu. "Actually, I rather look forward to it."

His heart pounded in his chest as she returned her gaze to his. "Then we're happy to come." Feeling like a fool standing there with his daughter in his arms, he knew he couldn't stretch the moment longer without looking like an idiot. "I should go."

Together, they walked toward the door, Veronica gathering their jackets. "Do you want me to carry these for you?"

"If you put them around Lulu, it should keep her warm for the quick walk to our quarters."

Quickly, she set about her task. "Hopefully she won't get too cold."

"I'll walk fast," Hank promised. "Goodnight, Suzie," he called out.

A "Goodnight," drifted from the kitchen sounding suspiciously like she'd been standing just inside the door listening to their conversation.

"That has to be the world's longest dishwashing," Veronica noted dryly. "It almost seems like she's avoiding us."

"Seems like it." Hank grinned back. "Not that I'm complaining."

"I'm not complaining either."

Hank found himself riveted to her lush lips pressed together as pink fanned across her cheeks. *Was she embarrassed, or was it the chilly air frosting around them?* She certainly seemed flustered. Hank wondered what it would be like to kiss her. Would her blush deepen?

"Goodnight, Hank."

Tonight, he would be left with nothing but his imagination to how that kiss would feel. "Goodnight, Veronica."

The air was crisp, snow heavy in the clouds as Hank's truck pulled to a stop. Lights hung from poles surrounding the rows of neatly lined firs and pines. He looked at the sign proudly proclaiming the Wilson's Christmas Tree Lot.

"I guess some things never change," he muttered.

"Is this where you normally get your tree from?" Veronica asked, pulling her gloves on.

"No, normally I get a permit and go into the national park and chop one down from there." He pushed his hat onto his head. "But this year I thought it might be easier to come here. Maybe next year Lulu can come out to the park and help pick one." Lulu smiled at him from the back seat where Suzie was undoing her car seat.

"I haven't been to one of these for years." Veronica pulled her knit cap down around her ears.

"How do you normally get your tree?" Hank opened the door to retrieve his daughter.

"My stylist selects it for me." Veronica came around the side of the car, Suzie at her heels.

"Doesn't sound very personal."

"No, but this Christmas I'm making sure every bit of it feels right." Veronica smiled, her eyes dancing merrily. Hank wondered if he felt right to her.

They walked up and down the rows of trees—tall, short, fat, thin, firs, pines. "Do you have an opinion on the type of tree you want?" he asked as Lulu skipped ahead of them, little hand reaching out to feel the foliage as she capered about.

"Not teeny tiny." Suzie skipped by to catch up with her sidekick.

"But not so tall that it won't fit," Veronica added, her brow furrowed thoughtfully as she gazed about. *Dear Lord, she was cute.* Her hand rested on a balsam fir. "Do you think this one would do?"

Hank crossed his arms and made a show of appraising the tree in front of him. "It has good foliage and shape." Veronica chewed on her bottom lip as she listened to him, for all the world appearing like his opinion was the definitive one. "Good color." He looked behind it. "Good size. I think you might have picked it."

She let her breath out in a cloud of frost and gave a delighted little jump. "Suzie, Lulu, we have a Christmas tree!"

HANK WATCHED as Veronica popped a piece of fudge in her mouth, enjoying the way she half closed her eyes as she savored the flavor sensation. "That might almost be my new favorite." She opened her eyes to stare at him, leaving him drowning in their depths. "Whoever thought of red velvet candy cane fudge is a genius."

"Peppermint swirl fudge is where it's at," declared Suzie, grabbing another piece off the plate in front of them.

"What about you, Hank? What's your favorite?" Veronica asked.

He looked around the café, the doorbell jingling merrily as patrons went in and out. It was a little bit of an institution in the small town. "I'm partial to a bit of maple bacon white chocolate myself." *And blue eyes.*

"I can't wait to get home and start decorating the tree." Suzie tapped the table excitedly. "But this fudge is worth the wait."

"Excuse me." The woman's voice was unfamiliar, but the Wyoming twang wasn't. "Are you Veronica Hughes?"

Veronica smiled graciously, placing the remains of her fudge delicately back on the plate. "Yes, I am. Have you tried the fudge?"

"Lordy me, yes, the double chocolate walnut is divine." The generously endowed middle-aged woman took a step closer, and a sense of intrusion buffeted Hank. He glanced quickly toward Veronica to see how she was reacting. The smile was still there and, except for some barely perceivable tightening around her eyes, she didn't appear worried. "Can we get a photo?"

"Of course we can." The words weren't even out of Veronica's mouth before the fan had thrust a phone into Hank's hands and barreled over to stand behind Veronica, wrapping her arms familiarly around her idol.

He quickly took the shot, hoping to get the woman on her way and out of Veronica's space. Dismayed, he realized they had caused a commotion, customers pointing at them and nudging each other. "Here's your phone." He almost tossed the device back at the woman. Blissed out on having met her idol, the woman floated away, and the crowd began to make their way over. Veronica was the picture of composure, except for the slight flaring of her nostrils. Little wonder. He found it overwhelming, and it wasn't even directed at him.

"Do you want to take our fudge and head home?" He began wrapping the confectionary up in paper napkins. "We can get a head start on the Christmas decorating."

Suzie's eyes lit up at the suggestion. "Lulu, we can get the tree decorated."

"Yes, please," Lulu said in her little girl voice. The one that still tugged at his heart. She didn't say much, but when she did, it always impacted him.

Hank scooped up the hastily gathered bundle and stood, the women following suit. Pushing himself through the crowd, the others tucked in behind him, he caught part of a muttered conversation. "—he must be her bit of rough. I can't wait to tell Wanda." He bit back a laugh. *I wish!* Focused on getting everyone out peacefully, he continued out the door and away from the gossipy woman.

THE TREE STOOD PROUDLY to one side of the roaring fireplace, the mantle of which had already been duly decked with stockings, carols once again playing in the background. Suzie had found a scented candle and the room now smelled of cloves, nutmeg, and cinnamon. As Veronica took a moment to stand back and admire their handiwork, she didn't think she'd ever seen a tree so utterly perfect before. Sure, there were clusters of baubles that Lulu had decided needed to be grouped on top of each other and patches that were sparse, but it was real. Unlike Christmas trees that she'd had since she'd become famous, this one had heart.

She almost missed Hank slipping quietly from the room. *What on earth is he up to?* Clearly having noticed it too, Suzie shot Veronica a quizzical look. She shrugged her shoulders as if to ask how she would know. Before it could go any further, he was back, holding something behind him.

"I reckon this isn't as fancy as you're used to, but if you don't have an angel or such, I thought this might do." He held out what he'd been holding almost tentatively.

Veronica's breath caught in her throat. In his hands was a rustic star made from old metal, spots of rust dotting its surface. It was obviously something he'd made. "Your pa is one very clever and talented man," she said to Lulu. "Maybe we should keep him around." There was a spark of some indefinable emotion as he gazed back at her. She might not recognize it, but the way she tingled, her body did.

A loud insistent knock sounded at the door, and Veronica jumped at the sudden intrusion. Mystified, she stared at the others. Everyone she knew in this small town except for Marvin was in this very room. "Hank, are you expecting anyone?"

The gleam dulled in his eyes as the moment so tangible before evaporated into thin air as he made no attempt to move. "Nope."

"Okay, kids." Suzie pushed herself to her feet. "You know, the easy way to solve this problem is to answer the door," she admonished as she made her way over to do just that. "I mean, how hard is it?" A gasp of stunned horror escaped her at the sight on the other side.

Confused, Veronica jumped to her feet, Hank moving protectively to stand between the danger and her, but not before she caught a glimpse. Anton.

"Veronica, who is this?" Hank looked ready to leap into battle.

Anton pushed past Suzie, giving her a dirty sideways glance as he did so. "You always did like treating the servants like they were special. Shouldn't this one be out in the barn before he can make a mess?" he sneered at Hank.

A vein bulged dangerously on the side of Hank's neck. "This is my ex-fiancé," she quickly explained. Embarrassed,

Veronica hated the way Hank's eyes flashed with disappointment when they darted to hers.

"Actually, that's what I'm here to talk about."

Anton took her limp hands in his, and she snatched them away. "There's nothing to talk about."

Not at all dissuaded, he continued as if her rejection hadn't happened. "We both made mistakes."

"Do you want me to throw him out?" Hank looked ready to forcibly remove him from the house.

Anton sneered at him. "I see you've made a few more than I have, Veronica." He reached out and stroked her cheek. "But I'm willing to forgive and move on so we can have a life together. One that we deserve in the bright lights, not here in some backwards town you've decided to hide in. This isn't worthy of you and your talents."

His audacity struck her horrifyingly mute, her body unmoving as he caressed her cheek. Slowly, she came back to life and moved sharply away, but not before she saw the anger burning in Hank's eyes.

"Come on, Lulu, it's time we head back to our quarters where we belong." The little girl, uneasy in the tense currents that now muddied the earlier happier vibe, moved to cling tightly to his denim clad leg. Hank pulled her in close.

"Please, Hank, you don't have to go." Veronica's heart sank when he didn't even bother to look her way as he left.

She didn't even feel Anton press his lips to her cheek or hear his words as she processed the loss. "I knew you would see sense."

How had her Christmas fantasy become a nightmare?

Suzie glared across the room at the man currently making himself at home in front of the fire. "Why the heck is he still here?"

Veronica sighed, sipping her cup of cocoa. "Because I can't just throw him out in the cold."

"Of course you can. If you need help with his bags, I'll toss them out for you."

"He said he cleared his schedule to come out here and make things right. He said we promised to spend Christmas together." Strange that now she didn't feel anything at all when she thought about him.

"This is the man who broke up with you and let you deal with the paps. I say we kick him out and let him deal with the coyotes. Seems like a fair swap to me."

Veronica set her mug down. "I'll talk to him."

"Fat lot of good that will do. You're better off telling him. Even then, my vote is to get Hank to come and throw him out." Suzie's eyes narrowed at the thought. "I'm not sure who would enjoy that more, Hank or me."

Shaking her head at her friend's ferocious words, she

walked over to Anton. The man who had been her fiancé, the two of them appearing to lead the perfect life. But with distance, she'd realized she didn't even know the man. Not really. "Anton, I appreciate you wanting to come here and talk, but really, there's nothing left to say. I admit, at the time, it stung that you decided to end it, but now, I have to give you credit. You were the one brave enough to call it quits, and it really is for the best." Her hand gently smoothed out each of the stockings hanging on the mantle as she spoke. *Veronica. Suzie. Lulu. Hank.*

"Give me some time. I promise your feelings will change." *Why wasn't the man listening?*

"I doubt they will."

Anton stood and walked up until he was behind her, his hand closing over hers and firmly removing it from the stocking that it had halted on. *Hank.*

"Then you've got nothing to lose by giving me a chance." How had she ever thought he was handsome? The way he looked at her, posing like he was in a movie, he just looked fake.

"You can stay until you arrange a flight back to LA." Suzie started waving in the background. *Cool your jets, I'm getting rid of him as fast as I can.*

He smiled smugly. Clearly he thought that would give him ample time to win her over.

"I see you're busy." Veronica jerked away from Anton at the sound of Hank's voice. "I'll come back some other time."

"I think you'll find she'll be busy then, too." Anton smirked at the cowboy.

Veronica glared at Anton, frustration boiling in her belly. "I'm not busy now. At least, not with anything that I really want." Suzie gleefully covered her mouth at the rebuttal. "Hank, Anton is only here until he can find a way to get back to LA."

Hank's expression looked like it had been carved from pure granite. "You don't need to explain anything to me. I'll come back some other time." He spun on his heel and strode from the room.

Veronica stared at his departing back open-mouthed. *Stubborn man. If he would just listen.* Frustrated, she retrieved her now cold cup of cocoa from the table and headed to the kitchen. "Suzie, feel like a drive into town for some shopping?"

"You had me at getting away from that jerk." Suzie narrowed her eyes at Anton as he sat back down, unperturbed by the discord he'd created. "The shopping is just the icing on the cake."

❧

SHOPPING in the small town was as polar opposite as you could get from Rodeo Drive. Here the shops nestled against each other like old friends, completely at ease with their flaws and age. Veronica loved it. Each store was a new little treasure to discover, some crowded to overflowing, a jewel that needed to be savored, others straight and to the point. Judging from the sheen in Suzie's eyes, she was enjoying it as much as Veronica was. And it might just be a coincidence, but in the last few shops, a lady seemed to always arrive just after they had.

"Suzie, have you noticed the woman over there?"

Her friend glanced over her shoulder at the woman. She seemed to be in her mid-twenties. "The one with the bad hair extensions and a fondness for over-contouring?"

Veronica quickly smothered her giggle. "Yes, that's the one. Do you think she's following us?"

Her friend shrugged, turning her attention back to the reindeer toy she held in her hand, pressing a button. A little chocolate pebble came out of the toy's rear end. "Oh, I need to get this for some people I know back in LA." Suzie added it to her bundle. "If she's a fan, she should just ask for a pic instead of creeping around."

The spark of holiday spirit she'd so carefully nurtured since she'd left the ranch evaporated. Veronica loved her fans, she really did, but right now, all she wanted to do was be left alone. At least until she could figure out how to get Anton to leave and Hank to look at her the way he had before her ex had shown up.

"Suzie?"

"You want to leave, don't you?" Her friend looked at her in perfect understanding that came from long years of knowing each other.

"I think we can do the rest of our shopping another day."

Suzie glanced over at the lady, still hovering in the shop. "Just let me pay for my things and we can blow this joint."

Love flowed through her. "Suzie?"

Her friend cocked her neon green head. "Yeah?"

"You're the best."

"You better believe it."

LULU WAS SPRAWLED out on the patchwork comforter that covered the sofa, involved in some sort of play with two dolls. Hank had strung some Christmas lights about the room to make it look more festive and she'd helped put glitter on some paper stars he'd cut out. There was a light knock at the door and somehow he knew that she'd be standing on the other side. He hated how much she affected him, especially now that she was more out of his reach than ever.

"Can I please come in?" asked Veronica, holding a cookie tin in her hands like a shield.

"It's your ranch." Didn't he just sound like a sullen little kid.

"That's not fair." She glided in like a fairy queen, somehow majestic and fragile all at once.

"It's true." Dang, he needed to shut his mouth.

"These are your quarters. You have the right to allow or not allow anyone you like here." She knelt beside Lulu, opening the lid of the container. "Suzie made these for you." Excited, the little girl dropped her dolls to give her friend a hug before reaching a hand in to collect a treat. Hank wasn't sure quite what it was, but from the quick glance he managed to get, it looked chocolatey. Satisfied that Lulu was occupied, Veronica straightened, her eyes never leaving his once. "I want to explain. About Anton."

"You don't need to explain anything to me." He felt an instant of squeezing hurt.

"I didn't know Anton was coming, and as soon as he can book travel back to LA, he's leaving. There's nothing there between us."

"It sure as heck didn't look that way to me." The way her ex had been touching her … well, it had made his hands itch to make him stop.

"He made his move, and he wants me to give him another chance, but what we had, it's over. There's nothing there. Not for me, at least, and there's nothing he can do or say that will change my mind." Veronica stepped in closer. He could smell her fancy perfume. It was heady, not the usual light floral that he usually associated with fragrance. "You're my friend and I thought maybe—" She dropped her gaze. She was so close he could see the sheen on her bottom lip where her tongue darted out nervously. "I thought that there might be something between us." There was the barest of pauses before she rushed on as if afraid that she would lose her nerve. "Or maybe the start of something."

Hank pressed down hard on the pad between this thumb and index finger, digging his nail in. Pain greeted his action. Good, he wasn't dreaming this. Veronica Hughes was standing in front of him saying that she had been feeling what he had. His heart pounded in his chest, and he was amazed that she couldn't hear it. Slowly, he reached out his hand to clasp hers, bringing it to his chest. Veronica's eyes widened as she felt the beats through his shirt.

"Veronica." His voice came out in a husky whisper.

A sharp series of knocks sounded on the door. "You've got to be kidding me," exploded Hank. "Again? I've learned from last time. I'm not answering that."

Veronica's brows furrowed as she pulled her hand out of his grasp. "It's cold out there. What happens if it's someone who needs help?"

"The only other people on this ranch besides us in here are Suzie and Anton. Suzie is smart enough to head on back to the lodge if we don't answer, and frankly, I don't care what happens to Anton." Visions of a blue-lipped shivering Anton caused the corners of his mouth to stretch into a pleased smile.

By now the knocks had evolved into pounding. *Someone definitely wanted in.* "Hank, you need to answer that. Whoever they are, they aren't going away." Veronica folded her arms across her chest as she gave him her best schoolteacher look. But he'd never had a teacher look as sexy as her when he'd gone to school, that's for sure.

"Fine. But as soon as I send them on their way, you and me are getting back to what we were talking about."

Veronica offered a sudden arresting smile. "Deal."

He stared at her a moment longer before striding across to the door and yanking it open. "What's with all the racket?"

Hank stopped, poleaxed by the woman standing in front of him. "Molly?"

"Are you going to invite me in?" Lulu's mother asked coolly as if the last time he'd seen her hadn't been her abandoning their child with him.

A gambit of emotions pummeled him, anger winning out. "What are you doing here?"

"Hank, who is it?" Veronica asked tentatively, coming to stand beside him. "You're the woman who was following Suzie and I around at the shops today."

His eyes narrowed at that little tidbit. "Molly, I'm going to ask again. What are you doing here?"

"If you let me in, I'll be more than happy to explain." Molly flickered a cold glance to Veronica. "Alone."

Veronica turned incredulous eyes to him. "This is Lulu's mother?"

"She gave birth to her, if that's what you mean." Hostility rang through every word.

"And raised her while you were off living the rodeo life." Molly looked bored. "If we're keeping score."

Veronica glanced over her shoulder where Lulu was back to playing with her dolls, oblivious to the adults. Turning back to him, she rested a hand gently on his arm, Molly's eyes narrowing at the sight. "I think I should go. You both clearly need to talk." Brushing past Molly, she made a dignified exit. Molly, seeing her opportunity, made her way in.

"She's grown," Molly noted as she took off her coat. "Hi, baby, do you remember Mommy?"

Lulu looked at her curiously. "Mommy?" Hank wasn't sure if she was repeating the name because it was familiar to her or because she genuinely remembered Molly.

"Yes, baby. Mommy." She sat down on the sofa and pulled Lulu into a hug. "Mommy's missed you."

"You have a funny way of showing it, what with not

calling or anything." Darn right he was mad.

"I had to get my head together."

"And while you've been getting your head together, Lulu and I have been living our lives. And as you can see, we've been doing just fine." More than fine. They were happy.

"Lulu is a lucky girl that you're her daddy. This time that I've had away from her, I realized what was wrong before. We weren't a family. That's what Lulu deserves."

Hank's breath burned in his throat. "But you left her."

Molly gazed over their daughter's head to look at him with wounded eyes. "Isn't that what you did to us all the time?" Guilt doused his anger. "You had none of the responsibility. You just left it all to me. Swooping back into town when you had time to play at being a parent before handing her back to me."

Remorse gnawed at his guts, and he hung his head. "I was providing for my daughter."

Molly smiled at him sadly. "You and I weren't exactly planning on being parents and certainly not together. But I don't regret Lulu."

Hank reached out and gently stroked his daughter's head. "Neither do I."

"We never really gave being a family a proper go, and I think we both owe it to Lulu to at least try. I'm staying in a motel in town. I came here to spend Christmas as a family." She gave Lulu another squeeze before releasing her to stand. "I know it's getting late, and I don't want to intrude for too long tonight. But I will be back tomorrow, and we can talk more then." She reached out to squeeze his arm, the gesture eerily similar to Veronica's from moments earlier. "Please think about what I said."

Hank watched her walk out the door. Mind whirling, he gathered his daughter up in his arms. "Lulu, Daddy loves you, but darn if he knows what to do."

Staying away from Veronica had been one of the hardest things Hank had ever had to do, but he didn't know what to say to her. *Hey, Veronica, Lulu's mom wants us to be a family and I'm the crazy guy who wants to give his daughter the world, but I don't know if I can give her that.* Knowing that he needed to end his own self-inflicted torture, he trudged over to the lodge. Familiarity meant that he didn't knock. Veronica and Suzie had both been quite firm when they'd said that anytime he needed to, to just come on in.

He opened the door and entered, the warmth fanning across his exposed face, and he slipped his boots from his feet. Standing in his sock clad feet, he could only stare dumbfounded at the change that had been wrought in the room. Gone was the fresh fir they'd selected together, replaced now with a silvery white spruce covered in blue and white ornaments, a large, bedazzled angel on top. The stockings had disappeared, boughs and berries in its place.

"What the blazes have you done here?"

Anton turned around smugly, a small bespeckled man

beside him. "Just taking out the trash." He threw a pointed look to where the star that Hank had spent his spare time in the evenings crafting poked out of a trash can. "Kieran here almost had a heart attack at that cheap, nasty thing." Anton shuddered in mock horror.

Veronica, Suzie, and Lulu walked in, laughter floating in with them full of merriment and magic. As one, they stopped dead. "What have you done?" breathed Veronica.

"Made sure that you are surrounded with beautiful things, my dear." Anton smiled, his perfect Hollywood teeth gleaming.

"It does make me wonder why you're still here, if that's the case," Suzie said.

Hank knew there was a reason he liked Suzie. Lulu's bottom lip began to tremble. "Don't like," she wailed before hiding her face in the legs of Hank's jeans.

"Lulu, sweetheart, I promise we'll get it back to how it was. Suzie, would you please take her into the kitchen and get her some milk and cookies? At least, if that's okay with Hank."

Hank nodded, still furious at the gall of the other man. Somehow, the star being in the trash can tarnished it, taking away all the hope and love he'd made it with. Veronica's nostrils flared as she fixed her attention once again on Anton.

"I think—or at least hope—your motivation was from a good place, but we were quite happy with how we'd decided to decorate our lodge for Christmas. You had no right to change anything."

"Sweetheart, I'm only looking out for your best interest." Anton moved as if to grab hold of her arms.

Hank stepped closer to Veronica, his hands clenching by his side. "I think Veronica knows what she wants."

"I think that she needs to make sure she protects her

image. Once she loses interest at playing ranch, she'll return to her career, and I don't want to see her damage it."

Veronica raised her chin and glared at Anton through narrowed eyes. "I've been in this industry for a long time, even longer than you. I've paid my dues and made enough money to never have to work again if I don't want to or be told what to do by any man."

Something shifted in Anton's face, a flicker of craftiness quickly gone. The haughtiness of earlier was replaced with humbleness. "Veronica, I owe you an apology, it seems. I misread the situation, and for that I am truly sorry. I was only trying to look out for you and make you happy."

Hank swore he heard a muttered, "Then leave," from the kitchen, a smile ghosting his lips when the other man's mouth tightened. Clearly, he'd heard it too.

Veronica let out a long sigh. "Look, Anton. All I want is a nice peaceful Christmas the way I choose to have it. I appreciate you trying to do what you think is right, but I need you to stop doing it."

Anton hung his head. "I promise."

Hank thought he was going to gag. "Is it okay for Lulu to stay here for a while? There are some things I need to do."

Veronica looked at him, her eyes dimmer than he liked seeing them. This close to Christmas, they should be sparkling with excitement of the holiday season. "Of course. Is there anything I can do to help?"

"No, I just need to check on the stock and then finish up a few things in the barn." He threw a threatening glare at Anton which the other man ignored. "If you need anything, let me know." She nodded, a soft smile all he needed to know that she understood his offer. Turning on his heels, he strode back out into the cold and away from the warmth he felt whenever he was around Veronica.

Sᴜᴢᴇ ᴛᴏᴏᴋ another cookie from her plate. This one had Barbie pink, lime green and black swirled in a haphazard pattern. "Lulu, have I ever told you that I love your color choices?" The little girl shook her head, crumbs falling from her mouth as she reached for her glass of milk. "I can't believe that jerk came in here and ruined our stupendous decorations. If he doesn't put it all back together exactly how it was, I swear, I'm going to have his guts for garters." She took a bite from her cookie. "I tell you, Lulu, some people can't see value unless a price tag tells them. Now, what are we going to do about your father and Veronica?" Lulu shrugged, eyes wide. "We're just going to have to do some Christmas magic of our own. No way can we let those two not be together, and if I need to shove them under the mistletoe myself to get some yuletide sense into their heads, well, I'm just the Christmas elf to do it."

"Dᴀᴅᴅʏ?" Bundled up against the cold, Lulu held out a plate of cookies.

"We thought you might need a snack." Suzie hunched her shoulders into her coat. "Brr. Snow seems great when it's fake on a movie set, but I can tell you, there's a reason I like living in LA."

"I don't think it would feel like Christmas if there wasn't snow." Hank held out his arms, and his daughter snuggled into them, settling onto his lap while still cradling her precious cargo. With his free hand, he put down the spanner he'd been working with. He wasn't sure when the tractor had last been checked and he didn't plan on letting it go any longer, not on his watch. "I think a snack is an excellent idea."

Suzie pulled up an overturned bucket. "Christmas is almost here, and except for the tree shopping"—Hank snorted at the reminder of what had happened to their tree—"and present shopping, we haven't done many Christmassy things."

Hank held up his cookie. "I've eaten plenty of sugar cookies."

"And fudge," Suzie added. "But I was thinking something special with Lulu."

"I guess I haven't taken her on a sleigh ride." Now that Hank thought about it, he knew his daughter would love it. Maybe Veronica would like to come too. If they could ever stop walking on eggshells around each other.

"And Veronica loves Christmas, maybe she could do with a little holiday cheer, too."

Hank's smile broadened. Looks like Suzie had the same idea as him. "I reckon she could."

Suzie returned his smile. "Well then, I think our work here is done. If you need us, we'll be back at the lodge coloring."

A quick hug and kiss from Lulu that stole even more of his heart, and then he was left to his own devices, his mood buoyant.

"I think it's a wonderful idea," Molly said. *What was with that woman? Was she just skulking about waiting to jump out of the shadows?* "Lulu will love it when we take her."

"I don't think you coming was discussed." His joy plummeted to the ground at his ex's sudden appearance.

Molly's mouth pinched. "Hank, a sleigh ride is just what we need. A Christmas memory for our little family."

Visions of him and Veronica with Lulu nestled between them with warm blankets over their laps gliding through the snow to jingling sleigh bells evaporated. He thought about

Lulu, what he wouldn't do to make her happy. He'd let her down last time, but this time he'd give her the family she deserved.

45

"*A* sleigh ride? With a horse and everything?"

Veronica put her sock covered feet closer to the fire, her cup of eggnog warm in her hands. It had taken a full day to get everything removed and the threat of violence to get the location of their old decorations revealed, but she'd done it. She'd gotten her Christmas back, and now it just kept getting better. *A sleigh ride! Just like in A Christmas Carol!* Giddy at the thought of snuggling in the back of a sleigh with Lulu and Hank as bells jingled merrily and snow crunched under the horse's hooves, she couldn't help clapping her hands together.

"It sounds magical."

"I'm almost jealous that I'll be on a call with my agent about a movie I'm booked for and won't be able to come too. Maybe next time," Suzie deadpanned.

"Oh, Suzie." She knew her friend was making sure it was just her, Lulu and Hank. "Thank you."

Smugly, Suzie added an extra dash of bourbon to her eggnog. "Just call me Elf Suzie." Her eyes flashed mischievously as she set the bottle back on the table. "Anyway, I think the two of you would make adorable children."

Veronica almost snorted her eggnog out of her nose. "Suzie! We met the man a month ago."

"Fine." Suzie tossed her brightly colored hair behind her shoulder. "Maybe it is a little too soon for children, but I bet the man knows how to kiss." Veronica could feel the burn of color across her cheeks. It wasn't like she hadn't thought about it. "Which actually brings me to the next thing we need to talk about," Suzie said matter-of-factly.

Veronica was almost too scared to ask. "There's more we need to talk about?"

"Yes. When the heck is Anton going back to LA?" Suzie sat back, resting her mug on her knee as she eyeballed her friend. "I know he's hopeless, but even he could manage to get a flight by now. And have you forgotten the heated helipads? Just order the man a helicopter and be done with it."

"I know." But it wasn't as easy as that. Every time she brought it up, Anton would beg her to give him—them—a chance. "After the Christmas decorations debacle, he started saying he knew how important the holiday season is to me and that he wanted to make it special." Glumly, Veronica stared into her mug. She knew what she should do, she just didn't have the heart to do it.

Apparently, her friend had no such concerns. "Did you tell him that him leaving would make it special for you?" Suzie raised her brows at her. "Just a thought."

"I can't. It would hurt his feelings." Veronica had even given herself a pep talk about it being like a Band-Aid and just ripping it off. Turns out she was a chicken.

Suzie stared at her like the imbecile she clearly was. "So, you're willing to spend Christmas miserable because you don't want to hurt the feelings of a guy who broke up with you and didn't even have the decency to do it in person but got your agent to do it?" Her voice was quite shrill by the end of it. "Veronica! Get a grip. We left LA, and you bought a ranch here in Wyoming because that guy had ruined your Christmas vibe and you *don't want to hurt his feelings*?" She covered her face with her hands. "I guess they don't call it the silly season for nothing."

Good Lord, Suzie could be dramatic. "I can't just kick him out."

"I could and would." Suzie dropped her hands from her face and looked Veronica square in the eye, her gaze drilling into her. Veronica squirmed, unused to being on the receiving end of such a look from her friend. "I'd even call the media and let them know it was happening." A smile ghosted her lips. "Because I'm good like that." All humor vanished from her face. "Especially if it means that I don't lose the guy I really want. The nice guy, the dependable guy, the no-tricks guy."

Veronica was the first to drop her gaze, confusion wrestling with a sense of longing. "I'm not even sure what I feel for Hank."

"But you do feel something for him. It seems like you and Hank are the only ones who are confused about it. The rest of us aren't."

Startled, Veronica frowned at her. "The rest of us?"

"Me and Lulu are all for it. Molly and Anton feel threatened as all heck about it."

"But I barely know him," she stuttered.

"You know enough to know what sort of man he is and that's a pretty good start."

Veronica found she couldn't argue with that logic. She stared into the flickering fire, the stockings once again returned to their rightful place, all their names in a row. From the corner of her eye, her attention was captured by the tin star high on the tree. So Suzie was right. But now what did she do?

"Are you busy?" Hank poked his head into the library.

Veronica looked up from the script she was marking up with her notes. "Not at all." She smiled at him warmly. He really was a handsome man. Rugged and earthy and as far from the Hollywood pretty boy as humanly possible. "In fact, I'm thankful for the break."

"I was wondering if it was all right if I finished up early today. They have this sleigh ride and I thought maybe I'd take Lulu."

A frisson of excitement sparked in her. It was happening. He was going to ask her out. "Suzie was telling me all about it. It's a pity she can't come."

Hank looked down at the floor for a moment before lifting his gaze. "Um, I was hoping that maybe she hadn't said anything."

The big softie had wanted to surprise her. Butterflies fluttered in her belly. "Oh, I'm sure she didn't mean any harm."

"She probably didn't, and when she left, I'm sure she thought it would be fine to say something."

Veronica's happiness turned to ice. "But now it's not?"

His finger tapped restlessly against the door frame. "It's just that Molly also had the same idea and, well, Lulu hasn't spent much time with her mom since she's been in town."

She knew her smile was brittle, a mask so thin it would crack if she needed to hold it for much longer. "Lulu will have a wonderful time." She ran a trembling finger over the script. "I was going to say that I'm busy too, unfortunately, but it's now worked out for the best after all."

Hank nodded with a taut jerk of his head. *Why was he*

acting all offended when he was the one to change the plan? "I'm sure she will. I'll make up the extra time over the week."

"Hank, don't worry. I won't dock your wages. Go enjoy spending some Christmas time with your daughter. She'll love it." Veronica tried hard to not think about her mother who would be there too. It was none of her business.

"Thanks." He looked like he wanted to say more. Gosh, how she wanted him to say more. With another nod, he left her to stew alone in regret with her script. *Merry Christmas to me.*

LULU'S CHEEKS WERE ROSY, her breath frosty in the air as her wide eyes took in everything from her snug place between them, blanket firmly in place. The bells from the heavy gray horse's harness jingled exactly like all of the Christmas carols promised as the sleigh glided along the snow to the steady accompaniment of crunching hoofbeats. Molly's attention was firmly on her mobile phone, taking pictures of herself and posing.

"Molly, I give. Why on earth do you want us to be a family?"

She put her phone down to stare at him. "I'm Lulu's mother. Why wouldn't I want us to be a family?"

He could already see in her expression the need to return to her device, the need to check how many likes she'd already garnered. "You dropped Lulu off like she was a bag of clothes. You didn't call once while she was with me, and this was the little girl you carried in your belly, who you cared for the first few years of her life. Heck, you lingered in the shadows to eavesdrop on a conversation rather than step forward and spend time with your daughter. You talk about family, but you're here with us and you aren't even hugging your daughter. What kind of mother does that? It's clear you don't want me, and I'm so fine with that, but I don't care about me. Why play games with Lulu?"

A canniness he never noticed flickered in the depths of her eyes, almost chilling in its ruthlessness. "Oh, fine," she huffed. "The money's hit my account and the agent has already helped raise my profile. I guess there isn't anything they can do about it now."

She might as well have been speaking Greek. Hank could only stare at her mystified. "What?"

Molly rolled her eyes skyward. "It's simple. I got a call from a PI who asked me some questions and if I know you. I told him yes, and he said that he knows someone who would like to talk to me and was willing to make it worthwhile."

"Worthwhile?"

Again, she rolled her eyes. "Pay me, obviously. Anyway, I met this man, and he wants to help me get famous, be an influencer, and he's even willing to pay me money—big money—and all I have to do is come here and play happy family with you for a couple of weeks."

Suspicion cut through the cloud of disbelief. "What was this guy's name?"

"I can't remember. I haven't heard from him again once he set me up with an agent."

"Try," Hank ground out. Lulu, catching the undercurrents swirling around, leaned in closer, seeking comfort from him. He wrapped an arm around her, snuggling her in tight.

"Oh, I don't know. Basil? Ginger? Something like that."

Hank permitted himself a withering glance. Fury clouded his vision as he leaned forward and tapped the driver on the shoulder. "Sir, if you would be so kind as to take us back. This sleigh ride is over." *How could she do this to her daughter?* And he'd almost been willing to fall for it, to give Lulu the family he knew she longed for. "Molly, I will never stop you from seeing Lulu, but I won't let you hurt her."

"Fine by me. It's not exactly good for my image to have a kid."

Hank kissed the top of Lulu's head. "Driver, if you could stop, please." The sleigh came to an abrupt halt. "Get out."

"Excuse me?" Molly gaped at him. "We're nowhere near the car."

"It's not that far, and the walk might teach you some humility. Now, get out."

She glared at him as if testing his resolve. Something in his flinty gaze must have told her not to push it. Flinging the blanket off her, she stepped from the sleigh. As they drove off, Hank didn't even bother looking back. He'd seen enough. And the worst part had been when she'd talked about not having a kid. She hadn't seemed that upset at all. For him, losing Lulu would be like losing a limb—something he didn't think he would ever be able to get over.

The smell of diesel, straw, and stockfeed filled Veronica's nostrils as she entered the barn. She wasn't sure what time Hank would be back, but she knew he always did a check of the barn in the afternoon. It wasn't like she'd know if something was wrong, let alone know how to fix it, but she wanted to do her part. It was her ranch, after all.

She trailed up the laneway where stalls had been built, currently standing empty. Maybe when it warmed up, she could ask Hank to get some horses. *How cute would Lulu look on a little Palomino pony?* Maybe she could call Marvin and find out if he could have one delivered by Christmas. *Imagine her face when she woke up and found a pony under the tree.*

Slow heavy footsteps sounded behind her. "I'm surprised to see you out here." Hank's gravelly voice sent goosebumps dancing across her skin.

"Not as surprised as I am to see you. Aren't you meant to be all sleigh-bells-a-ringing?"

His mouth twisted as he rubbed the back of his neck. "Well, it turned out to be more ex-girlfriend-a-leaving."

"Molly left? Why? More importantly, where's Lulu?" Dread sickened her. *Had Molly taken Lulu?*

"She's with Suzie. I came round the lodge to see you and she told me you were out here, as she said it, playing rancher." A small smile lightened his expression as he looked her over. "You don't look dirty enough to be a rancher."

Indignant, she drew herself up to full height. "I'll have you know that I can be dirty when I want to be."

Veronica's face flamed hotly when she realized what exactly she'd said. Hank's guffaws didn't help either. "Anytime you want to show me, I'll be more than happy to give you my expert opinion," he finally managed.

She allowed herself a laugh. "Well, I guess if I ever find myself in the position of needing advice on the subject, I'll be sure to let you know." Her feminine ego was definitely flattered by the hungry look he cast her way. "So, didn't Molly like the sleigh ride? Is that why she left, to go back to the motel?"

"The problem is that Molly doesn't like anyone but herself. And that means she only wants to do what Molly wants to do, and that doesn't include being a mom to Lulu or being with me." His mouth quirked again. "Not that she's the woman I want to be with either, so in that matter, at least, I think I dodged a bullet."

Veronica swallowed hard against the shock of his words. *How could a mother leave her child? Especially Lulu?* Breathless, her mind caught up with the last of his words. *Not the woman I want to be with.* Was he admitting that she was the one he wanted? He looked down at his hands for a minute, the silence stretching between them.

"But maybe that's a conversation for another day. I see you've got the ranch under control. I think I might go get my daughter—if she'll leave Suzie, that is—and have a daddy-daughter evening with a Christmas movie." For a moment, a wistful expression stole over his face. Did he want to invite her? And then it was gone. "I guess I'll be seeing you in the morning."

"See you then." Veronica watched the broad-shouldered man turn and walk away, a steady cadence to each step taking him further from her. Molly was a fool walking away from a man like Hank. The question was, would Veronica be a fool too?

~

"I DON'T SEE why it's a problem. It doesn't seem that hard at all," Anton whined.

Suzie had her hands firmly planted on her hips. "You know what's not hard? Getting on a plane and getting some sushi in LA and never coming back."

"All right." Veronica held her hands up, playing peacemaker. "Everyone calm down. What's going on?"

Anton wrinkled his nose at her. "You're very earthy smelling."

"Yeah, that's what happens when you're on a ranch." Veronica looked at Suzie. "What did I interrupt?"

"This idiot demanding that I magic up some sushi because he wants some." Suzie angrily gestured out the window. "He does know it's snowing right? Where the heck does he want me to get fresh tuna? And let's not even get started on him treating me like I'm some sort of servant. I'm here as a friend and guest, which is more than I can say for him."

Veronica sighed. She wished she could say it so bluntly to Anton, but the fact of the matter was that she'd once cared about him, and she just couldn't bear to hurt his feelings. No one deserved to be alone on Christmas. "Anton, please stop ordering Suzie around."

"Fine. I'll have my PA send some out." Anton smiled seductively. "Maybe he can add a little something for you as well."

"You're more delusional than I thought if you think Veronica is going to be won over by some California rolls," Suzie muttered. Veronica privately agreed with her.

"I have some calls I need to make." And with that, Anton waltzed from the room.

"Good riddance." Suzie shook her head disbelievingly. "I can't believe you lived with that man and were going to marry him." She cocked her brightly colored head to one side, a feathered earring dangling. "Actually, now that I think about it, why were you ever upset that it was over?"

Veronica snorted as she went to pour herself a cup of coffee. "Let's just say that I'm questioning a lot of things since I left LA."

Suzie silently held her mug out for a refill. "At least you're starting to come to your senses. Now, that next step is to kick him out."

She handed the creamer to her friend. "We talked about that."

"And I was hoping you'd see the errors of your ways. So let me lay it out for you again. Don't be selfish."

"What!?" exploded Veronica. "I'm the least selfish person I know."

"That's true, but Hollywood isn't exactly renowned for people thinking of others."

"Suzie!"

"Just kidding. Sometimes you're so nice it makes my teeth hurt. But seriously, don't ruin Christmas by having some sort of misguided guilt toward Anton. The man does not deserve it."

Veronica stared down at her coffee, suddenly wishing

she'd poured something a little stronger. "I'll talk to him, I promise."

Suzie wrinkled her nose. "I won't say the obvious, but I'll believe it when I see it." Her eyes gentled with understanding. "Look, one of the things I love most about you is your heart, but seriously, you need to put yourself first. Christmas is a time for new beginnings, a time to take a chance and to be surrounded by loved ones." A determined glint set a ferocious cast to her features. "And if your past won't leave this ranch, I'm more than happy to kick him out for you."

THREE DAYS TILL CHRISTMAS

It was her Christmas. He'd never liked Christmas when they were together, so why did he care now? Why did she even care about his feelings? He hadn't. Veronica picked up the bottle of bourbon sitting on the table beside her mug of eggnog, adding a generous dose to it. It was time. Anton had to go. He'd taken advantage of her good nature for the last time. Normally, sitting here with the lights on the Christmas tree sparkling merrily as the fire roared, the air smelling of cinnamon and nutmeg, she'd feel like she was wrapped up in the yuletide spirit. Instead, not even her favorite Christmas sweater could save her mood.

She picked up her cup before setting it down again. *Argh, I hate conflict.* Veronica swallowed, forcing some steel into her spine. *It had to be done. Time to put on my big girl panties.* She grabbed the bottle of bourbon from the table to take a healthy swig before standing, the liquid blazing a fiery trail down her throat when it left a delicious warmth in her belly. It was time.

She found him where he'd spent much of his time holed up in the guest room he'd commandeered as soon as he'd arrived. It had struck her as odd that, for someone who had professed his love for her and begged for second chances, he'd also spent quite a bit of time away from her. Maybe he only loved her in small doses.

She knocked on the door, frowning at the footsteps and rustling. *What on earth was he doing inside?* Leaning forward, she pressed her ear to the door, jumping backwards in alarm when it opened. Straightening, she prepared to launch into her prepared eviction speech when she caught sight of the state of his room. Clothes were in piles on the bed, suitcases open and in varying states of packed. *He was leaving.*

"Veronica, you've saved me a trip to find you." Anton waved a scarf in her direction. "But it appears I'm going to have to miss spending Christmas with you after all."

She stood there waiting for a sense of hurt, disappointment—honestly, anything—but there was only a sense of relief and slight confusion at why now. "I'm sure it's for the best."

"I'll say. I've been cast in the latest Tyrone Quentin film, and it is imperative that I start preparing for the role immediately. It's an adaptation of a memoir and I want to be faithful to the source material."

She couldn't control her burst of laughter at the irony of her earlier pep talk. "I thought you'd come here to pledge your undying devotion, and the first role that comes your way, you're gone. Poof." She blew on the palm of her hand.

Anton stopped his relentless packing, an introspective cast stealing across his features. He set down the silken pair of boxers he'd had in hand and turned fully to face her. "You know Herb arranged it, right?"

It didn't surprise her. He was, after all, both of their agent. "The new role?"

"Yes. My last film was a flop, and since you and I broke up, well, the auditions have already started to dry up or at best are for supporting roles. Herb suggested that I come out here, and you know how he can be when he suggests something. He promised me a good role if I did."

It really should sting more than it did. *Maybe the bourbon had kicked in?* "Why would he do that?"

"Because he didn't want his superstar to disappear into the wilds of Wyoming."

Veronica gave a brittle laugh. "I imagine he quite liked the idea of the headlines too, if you'd managed to do what he wanted. Anton Villas and Veronica Hughes rekindle their relationship with the help of a little Christmas magic."

The first genuine smile she'd seen Anton give in a long time made him look ten years younger and carefree. "I would say he'd hoped for something like that." He took her hands. "Look, I'm a selfish jerk and I know that. I guess maybe it was why I never could push harder for a reconciliation for us. Especially when I saw how you looked at that rancher. But seriously, you need to get a new agent. When I was in Herb's office the day I left to come here, I overheard him talking to a lady on the phone about your ranch hand. You seem happy here. I don't want Herb wrecking it for you."

Veronica gave his hands a gentle squeeze back. "Thanks for telling me. You know I don't hate you. In fact, there are some things we did together that I will look back on and smile at."

"That time I almost caused a red carpet wardrobe malfunction when I stood on the hem of your dress?"

"That wasn't one I was thinking of, but at least I can laugh about it now."

Anton gave her a gentle kiss on the forehead. "I'm going to finish packing and then go. Merry Christmas, Veronica. I hope you get what your heart desires."

Strangely, now she felt the sting of tears. Their breakup

had never had the closure it needed, and now she was ready to finally close that chapter and move on to a new one. "Merry Christmas, Anton. I know you're going to be amazing in your role. Now, I need to go. There's something I need to do."

Flying down the stairs, she almost barreled into Suzie coming back from outside where she and Lulu had been sledding. "Have you seen Hank?"

"Not since he left for town." Suzie searched her face. "Is everything all right?'

"It's never been better." She beamed at her friend as she took Lulu's chilly hands and did an impromptu jig. "I've never felt better. Did I mention that Anton is leaving? Today."

Stunned, Suzie stared at her before a wide smile split her face. "Why didn't you say so?" She joined their jig. "Merry Christmas to me. Is this why you wanted Hank?"

"I wanted to share the news with him, but it can wait. I mean, Anton hasn't left yet."

"And he didn't have to share the lodge with him the way I did. Really, I was the first person you should have told." A wicked smile crept over Suzie's face. "I wonder how long it will take Hank to notice he's gone. Maybe we shouldn't tell him and just wait for him to notice himself."

"Is it wrong that I don't hate the idea?" Veronica felt a wonderful silliness creep over her.

"Then I say we go with it." Suzie picked up Lulu and twirled the giggling girl around. "I mean, we deserve some happiness after all."

Loretta looked bored. She pursed her overlined lips as she fixed her gaze balefully on him. "Look, honey, if you're not going to buy something, I need to go attend to other customers."

Hank's eyes darted between the earrings, the perfume, and the purse he'd gathered with Loretta's help. Nothing felt right. He'd had gifts chosen a week ago for Lulu and Suzie. But Veronica? Well, what did you get the woman who could pay cash for her own ranch, flew around on private jets, and regularly holidayed on islands?

"I'm sorry, Loretta, but I don't think I'll be taking anything. You've got such lovely things in here that I just can't decide. I'm sorry for wasting your time."

The exasperated sigh that had been brewing on her lips fell away to girlish simpering by the end of his words. "You can make it up to me, Hank, by taking me out to dinner. I hear Molly has left town."

Small town gossip. "She surely has, but I tell you, I'm plumb busy at the ranch this time of year. Especially with the nasty weather that's forecast for the new year. Best I don't make any plans until at least spring." Quickly grabbing his hat from the counter, he beat a hasty retreat before the determined Loretta could block his escape.

Hank pulled his collar higher up his neck when the bracing wind hit him as soon as he exited the shop. *No amount of cold was enough to risk getting tangled up with Loretta.* Pushing his hands deep into his pockets, he paused. Another flurry of snow and wind turned the streetscape into the inside of a snow globe, the Christmas lights and garlands dusted in white. Frustrated at his failure to select the perfect gift for Veronica, he worked off his excess energy by closing the distance to his truck with quick strides. *Maybe some Christmas inspiration would strike on the way home.* At least, he hoped so.

*D*arn, he should have made the wall straighter. Now no amount of shoring up the foundation would help the drunken lean, the roof threatening to fall off completely on that side. "Lulu, can you please pass the mortar?"

With a serious expression, she complied, her eyes willing him to make it right. Dipping his spatula into the icing, he applied a generous dollop to a discarded boiled candy and tried to wedge it underneath. Amazingly, it lifted the end of the wall a fraction, enough to at least stop the slide of the shingles.

"I think we saved it." Lulu smiled brightly at him. The light of that smile filled him to his very soul. Hank pulled her in and hugged her tightly. "I love you, Lu."

She giggled as he blew a raspberry on her tummy. "Luv you, Daddy." He didn't think he would ever get tired of that. "Lulu luv Ronica and Suzie."

"Well, let's just hope they love our creation." He picked it up, balancing it carefully, he didn't want it to suffer a catastrophic mishap so close to the finish line. "Now, Lulu, help Daddy with the door. We have a gingerbread house to deliver."

~

"You know, next year I think we should have a Christmas Eve cookie swap." Suzie held up a container of glitter. "More?"

Veronica looked into the mixing bowl filled with chopped hay, some grated carrots, a smattering of sequins, and a faint shimmer of glitter. "You can never have too much sparkle."

"Spoken like a woman after my own heart."

"Happy Christmas Eve, ladies." Hank greeted the room, his attention focused on safely transferring his cargo onto the kitchen counter. Once relieved of it, a goofy grin completely transformed his features. *This was the Hank he hid away most of the time,* she realized. Curiously, he peered into the bowl. "I don't think I want to eat that."

Suzie smacked his hand away. "If you did, I can guarantee you'd poop like a unicorn. This is for the reindeer." She put her head close to Lulu. "You did tell him about the reindeer food, didn't you?"

The little girl gave a little shrug. "Nope."

Suzie frowned. "Why not?"

"Surprise." The little girl grinned at her father. Hank beamed down at her.

Veronica's heart squeezed at the perfect moment, feeling almost like an intruder for being there, and then Hank looked over Lulu's head toward her and gave her a look that sent the thought fleeing before the warmth of his gaze.

"I just need to add a few more cookies to this plate and then I need someone to help pour a glass of milk for Santa." She made a show of looking around. "Are there any big strong cowboys who can help a lady out?"

Hank's rumble of laughter rang through the room. "I think I might be able to help, little lady." With deft movements, he retrieved a glass from the sideboard and filled it. "Now what?"

Veronica glanced over to Suzie. "Is the reindeer food ready?'

Her friend gave it a little shake under the light, peering intently into the bowl. "I think it's done."

"Great." Veronica knelt beside Lulu. "What should we do first? Put Santa's plate of goodies out, or some water and food for the reindeer?"

"Reindeer," the little girl replied earnestly.

"That's my girl." Hank proudly patted her daughter on the head. "A rancher always looks after the livestock first."

Together, they wandered out to the front porch, the Christmas lights twinkling against the frosty evening sky. The smell of snow was heavy in the air, the perfect white Christmas. Suzie held out her bowl to the little girl. "Do you think you can help me find just the right place to put this?" Lulu nodded enthusiastically. "How about here?" Suzie hovered over a chair.

"Too high." Lulu's face was a study of concentration.

"What about beside the door?" Veronica asked.

"No." Lulu looked around, her little hands on her hips. "There." She pointed to the edge of the porch near the steps. "Daddy?" There was a questioning note to her voice.

"Yes, Lu?" Hank knelt down beside her.

"Good?"

"Lulu, baby, I think that is the perfect place. Enough out of the weather, but easy for the reindeer to get to. As an added bonus, they won't mess up Veronica and Suzie's porch." Hank grinned up at them. Veronica didn't think her heart could beat any faster in her chest. Turns out she was wrong as he gently took his daughter's hand and gave it a kiss.

Lulu gave a decisive nod. "There."

Suzie placed the bowl down. "Well, reindeers, I hope you like your food. And if you need to warm up, there's always the helipads."

Veronica moved over, standing on the other side of Lulu as Hank rose to his feet, still holding her hand. Something small crept into Veronica's own hand. She looked down to find Lulu had claimed hers as well. It appeared that she was just as skilled at stealing hands as she was hearts. Tears threatened as Veronica swallowed the lump in her throat. Risking a glance, she found Hank gazing at her, a contemplative gleam to his gentle eyes. A tender smile curved his lips as he looked down to where their hands were linked with his daughter's before capturing her gaze again. Something profound shifted in Veronica. Standing on that cold porch, she felt all the Christmas magic she'd longed for swirling around her. Maybe her Christmas wish might just come true after all.

It was impossible to not feel sentimental as everyone sat in front of the Christmas tree, gifts being handed out. The sheer joy that shone from Lulu's face made this Christmas feel like it had an extra sprinkling of holiday cheer. It had started off when Suzie and Veronica, decked in matching Christmas pajamas, had answered the door to a shriek of pure excitement.

"They eat it!"

Opening the door had revealed Lulu wrapped up snug with a coat, jumping up and down where the reindeer bowl now laid precariously on its side, a few crumbs trailing from it.

Veronica held her hand out to the little girl. "Come and see what Santa did to the treats we left out for him." Once inside, she helped take off Lulu's coat to reveal that she was wearing matching jammies with the women and handed it to Hank. Veronica hadn't been able to help herself when she'd ordered sets for everyone. She'd be lying if she wasn't a little disappointed that Hank had already dressed for the day in jeans and a sweater. *Maybe next year?*

Together, they went into the hall where the plate had been left. The glass had a faint smug of cloudy white down the bottom, and all that remained of the cookies was one lonely crumb. "Old Santa must have been hungry," Hank said, looking over their shoulder.

Gosh darn, but he smelled good.

"And I think that's the last one," Suzie said, handing another present to Lulu and jerking Veronica back to the reality. "Um, Hank?"

"Yeah?" Hank looked guiltily at Suzie.

"Did you forget something?" Eyes open wide, she jerked her head toward Veronica. It dawned on her that she hadn't received anything from Hank. She told herself that it didn't hurt, but she had spent ages selecting the new Bluetooth speaker for him. Once she'd found out how much he liked listening to music while he worked, she knew she could do better than him just using his phone speaker.

He carefully slid Lulu off his lap, not meeting Veronica's eye. "Look, it's something stupid. I made something for you." Clearly, he was in no rush to actually hand it over. He coughed nervously. "I guess I'll go get it for you."

As the girls waited, Lulu happily cooed as she played with her new dollhouse. Suzie shrugged at Veronica as mystified as her. "What is he doing?"

She was just about to answer when Hank returned, his hands firmly held behind his back. Veronica could hear the paper crinkling as he nervously wet his lips. "Please don't laugh, or worse, be polite when you open it." He gave a boyish half smile. "Or, at least, don't do it while I'm here." Vulnerability lay bare beneath the light words.

This gift meant something to him. Hank thrust a poorly wrapped present complete with a lopsided bow into Veronica's hands. She didn't think she'd ever seen anything more perfect in her life.

Curious, Lulu had abandoned her toys for the moment and laid her hand on Veronica's arm. "Lulu see too."

"Of course." Veronica sat down on the sofa, and Lulu climbed up beside her, her hair glowing with the backlighting from the fire. Ever so carefully, she pulled back the paper to reveal a star, a twin to the one that once again broadly sat atop their tree. But this one was different. Carefully painted wording had been added. *May this star always guide you home. Love, Hank and Lulu.*

The edges of the star blurred as emotion fought to escape her. Her finger trembled as she gently traced the shape of the words. "It's…" She choked back her tears. "It's beautiful." She kissed the top of Lulu's head before rising slowly to her feet.

Hank stood waiting, a question shining as brightly as the star surely did as she closed the distance between. "Please don't cry. You have no idea what it does to me to see you cry." Tenderly, he reached a calloused hand out to wipe the tears that silently trailed down her face. "You have no idea what you do to me."

Veronica clasped the back of his hand where it rested on her cheek. "Maybe you can show me."

Her heart turned over at the tenderness in his gaze. "I'm out of practice. I might need to show you more than once."

Veronica's lips curved into a smile. "I think I might like that."

His lips were surprisingly gentle as they claimed hers, the kiss slow and thoughtful. His featherlight touch sent a shockwave through her, it was like her soul was claiming his. Surprised, she opened her eyes to see him staring down at her in shock. *Was it possible he'd felt it too?*

Her hand found its way to the back of his head, and she pulled him back into the kiss. As it deepened, she could have sworn she heard Suzie murmur, "I told you, Lulu. All they needed was a little Christmas magic."

And here in Wyoming with her rancher cowboy, she'd found it.

His hair was now prematurely as white as the snow that shone under the pale moonlight, but he was still as handsome as he'd ever been. Hank liked to say that it was the stress of being married to her and raising their kids that had done it. She knew he loved every minute of it.

The night was chilly but clear, the perfect Christmas Eve as Veronica's hand crept into his, and his large warm hand wrapped around hers. That feeling that had never left her after all these years descended over her. Home. Inside in the warmth, she could hear Lulu with the grandkids, home to the ranch for Christmas, their other children playing and laughing with their niece and nephew. All of them romping around in their matching Christmas pajamas—the family tradition that had started all those years ago.

Gently, she traced the names on the weathered star, more having been added as their family had expanded.

"Cold?" He could still make her heart beat faster with a single glance.

"A little. But with you here to keep me warm, I think I can last a little longer."

Laughing, he complied with her command and pulled her into his warm embrace, his arms still strong. "Better?"

"Much." She nestled her head into his chest. "No matter where I went or how many movies I made, I always knew how to find my way home." She peeked over his arm to the scene inside of the window. "And now the children do, too."

Hank's hand gently tilted her head back to his, the plain gold band glinting on his ring finger. "That they do. Merry Christmas, my love."

Their lips found their way together instinctively. She knew she would be able to find this man she'd been lucky to love and call her own for nearly three decades in a dark room. "I think it's time we get into our pajamas, too. The reindeer food and cookie swap aren't going to do themselves."

"I don't know." Hank tucked a strand of hair behind her ear. "If Lulu doesn't know what to do by now, there's no hope for her." His arms were still snug around her.

Veronica smiled up at him. "You might be right. What were you thinking?"

That devastatingly handsome smile of his flashed down at her. "One more kiss, maybe two."

"Well, it is Christmas Eve after all."

As his lips claimed hers again, she knew that he always had and always would be her guiding light, her Cowboy Christmas Star.

THE END

As an Indie Author, reviews help me get my books noticed. If you enjoyed reading Hank's and Veronica's story as much as I did writing it, please leave a review. It will make all the difference to me.

If you loved, *The Cowboy's Christmas Star,* sign up for my newsletter here to get free bonus's and exclusive news. Now, turn the page to discover *Her Reluctant Christmas Cowboy Star*

Suzie stared at the email. *The tenth anniversary of Luciano and Frankie's movie.* It couldn't be that long, could it? Gosh, she'd only been starting out in the business back then, barely twenty years old and filled with all the naivety of youth. Luciano and Frankie were so in love and now had children who were starting out in junior rodeos for themselves. Ash and Kirk Cooper had gone on to become Hollywood royalty and one of the most powerful couples in the industry. Savannah was still a rookie on the circuit, and Bryce followed her around like a tipsy puppy. Heck, Savannah had won the gold buckle three times now.

Suzie sighed. She would be coming off a three-month movie shoot in Nairobi and had hoped to go down to Veronica's ranch early for Christmas, but it had been years since they'd all been in the same room together. But dang, if it wouldn't be all sorts of fun. There were so many good memories. Especially that shy young cowboy who had come in as one of the extras so many years ago. He'd been all sorts of cute, even if he'd never quite managed to do more than smile at her. What was his name again? Greyson.

Yes, indeed. Greyson was definitely one of those good memories.

Her Reluctant Christmas Cowboy Star available on Amazon and in Kindle Unlimited here

ACKNOWLEDGMENTS

A debt of gratitude to my editor Rebekah Groves for her patience with me.

Another big thanks to Megan from Designed with Grace for her cover design.

To my amazing beta readers and street team, you guys rock and I couldn't do it without you. Special mention to Lisa and Cair.

And finally to my fabulous alpha reader Trixie Norman, for all the late nights of reading and endless questions about your thoughts.

Billionaire Hearts Ranch Series

The wounded cowboy billionaire

He had all the money in the world—and it wasn't enough to keep his life from falling apart…

Buy Now

The billionairess' cowboy

He broke her heart once. She's not about to let him do it again...

Buy Now

The billionaire's cowgirl

They were polar opposites who thought they had it all…until they met each other…

Buy Now

The cowgirl's fake billionaire marriage

There's one rule in their fake marriage--don't fall in love. But rules are meant to be broken...right?

Buy Now

A cowboy's riches (Prequel)

She's broken free and is ready to fly…or ride, as the case may be…

Buy Now

Billionaires Lonely Hearts Club

Red Dust and The Billionaire

Wild horses couldn't drag this couple to happily ever after…right?

Buy Now

Star Dust and The Billionaire

It'll take more than star dust and Hollywood magic to get *this* couple to happily ever after...

Buy Now

Gold Dust and The Billionaire

His friends can settle down, but *he* won't. Or so he kept telling himself...

Buy Now

The Brothers of Creekside Ranch Series

Levi

Levi and Bella's story

Pre Order Now

Amos

Pre Order Now

Elijah

Pre Order Now

Barrels and Hearts series

Available on Amazon and Kindle Unlimited

A Bull Rider's Paradise

The prequel to the Barrels and Hearts series. True love is only the beginning....of the story. Find out where it all began with Ana and Eduardo. Sometimes finding love is easy. It's keeping it that's hard.

Buy here

A Cowgirl's Dream

An Aussie cowgirl far from home. A handsome Brazilian bull rider. Can they have a rodeo love story of their dreams?

Buy Now

A Cowgirl's Heart

An Aussie cowgirl in need. Her childhood friend to the rescue. Can friendship turn into a love story?

Buy Now

A Cowgirl's Passion

One feisty cowgirl. One steadfast Brazilian bull rider. Will she see what is right in front of her?

Buy Now

A Cowgirl's Pride

An Aussie cowgirl from the wrong side of the tracks. A handsome equine vet. Can they find a way to have their happy ever after?

Buy Now

A Cowgirl's Love

A young Aussie cowgirl. A widowed rancher. Does age matter when it comes to love?

Buy Now

A Cowgirl's Movie Star

A fiery cowgirl with big dreams. A movie star far from home. When their two worlds collide, will their love be strong enough to hold them together or will they be pulled apart

Buy Now

A Cowgirl's Billionaire

A cowgirl adrift. A broken billionaire cowboy. Can he free himself from the past to be the man she needs now?

Buy Now

Cowboy Christmas Series

The Mistletoe Collection

Boots and Mistletoe

Cowboy boots, mistletoe, and a holiday do-over…

Buy Now

The Cowboy Under the Mistletoe

It'll take more than the magic of the season to help this grump find her happily ever after...

Buy Now

Mistletoe and the Billionaire's Cowgirl

He's the last man she wants this holiday season. Too bad he's exactly what she needs...

Buy Now

ABOUT THE AUTHOR

Edith MacKenzie or Eddie Mac to her friends is an author of sweet and wholesome contemporary cowboy romance. They say in literary circles to write what you know, and Eddie has certainly taken that to heart. Before embarking on a writing career, she trained horses professionally and brings that wealth of knowledge to her writing.

Now a mum to a boy and girl, as well as wife, she delights with her tales of strong cowgirls and their adventures in finding love. When not weaving the love stories of her characters, she enjoys hanging out with her family and animals, as well as reading, fishing and camping.

Just remember—once a cowgirl, always a cowgirl.

facebook.com/EddieMacAuthor
instagram.com/edith_mackenzie_author
amazon.com/Edith-MacKenzie
bookbub.com/profile/edith-mackenzie
twitter.com/edith_mackenzie

www.ingramcontent.com/pod-product-compliance
Lightning Source LLC
Chambersburg PA
CBHW030438120726
47903CB00003B/1016